Is Al Khizr still alive today?

Abdul Waheed

Is Al Khizr still alive today?

Abdul Waheed

Awarded to
Abdul Waheed
for publishing "Is (Al Khizr still alive today?,"

PUBLISHED AUTHOR
notionpress
CERTIFICATE OF PUBLISHING
We're proud to present this certificate of publishing to
Abdul Waheed
for successfully publishing
IS (AL KHIZR STILL ALIVE TODAY?,
on 20-01-2023
"A writer's life and work are not a gift to mankind; they're a necessity"~ Toni Morrison

Dedication

This book is dedicated to the memory of my late father Haji Ubairdur Rahman (Munna Bhai) and younger brother Abdul Hameed. May Allah Taala (God) give peace to his soul. Aamen.

Table of contents

Preface

An ancient person named Al Khizr has been special, whose mention has come in the Holy Quran. People of the Kabirpanthi group of Hinduism consider him as God, similarly there are different beliefs about him in different texts, some people also believe that he is alive even today.   Please read it and take advantage, if there is any shortcoming, please inform. Thank you,

Yours - Abdul Waheed, Barabanki, UP, India.

Date- 15/01/2023

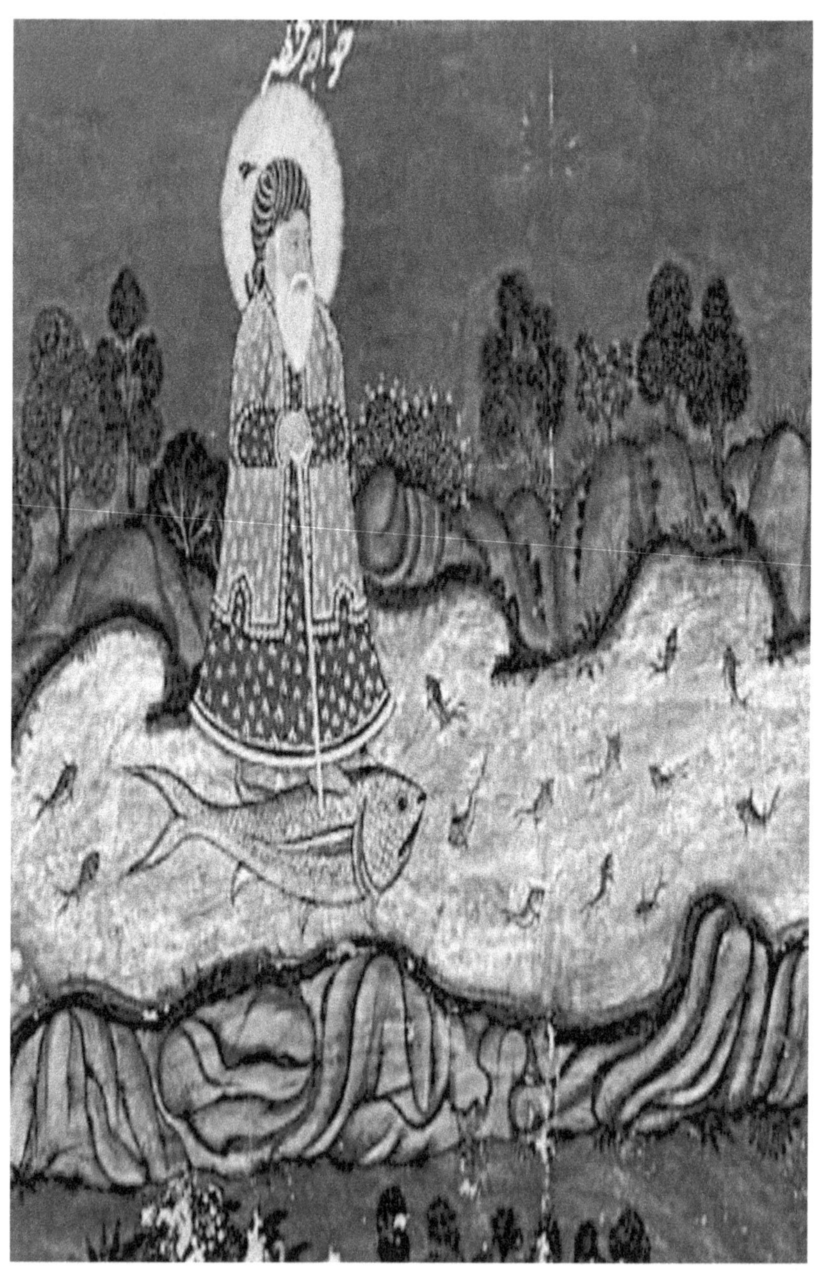

Is Al Khizr still alive today?

According to the Holy Quran, Al-Khidr is the servant of Allah with wisdom. In many texts, Khidr is described as a messenger, prophet, angel who protects the ocean, helps them in distress and imparts secret knowledge.

Some Muslim scholars believe that Alkhizr gets immortality by drinking nectar (Abe Hayat). Al-Khizr is still present on earth. He appears anytime, anywhere after listening to the call of the devotee and ends all the sufferings of the devotee and gives philosophy to the devotees. Devotees yearn to get salvation from him. According to Sufi saints, he must meet Alkhizr once in his lifetime. Devotees from many countries including India come in search of him once a year in Katargama village of Alkhizra in Sri Lanka.

Some people believe that Alkhizr means green. When the philosopher Saint Al-Khizr sits on a barren land, that land becomes green and fertile, that is why farmers, cattle herders worship him as a green sage or god of vegetation. When there is a famine, it is Al-Khijr who saves us from the water crisis, then he is also called Varun Devta. Wearing green clothes, this Baba gives darshan to many people, that's why he is also known as Green Mahatma.

There are many such figures in Iran who were replaced by Khizr in the process of Islamization. One of them is paradoxically a female figure, Anahita. The most popular temple in Yazd is dedicated to Anahita. In Zoroastrianism, for pilgrims to Yazd, the most important of the six Pirs is Pir-e Sabz ("Green Shrine"). The name of the temple is derived from the greenery of the foliage that grows around the sanctum. It is still a functional temple and the holiest site for present-day Zoroastrians living in Iran. Each year from June

14–18, thousands of Zoroastrians from Iran, India, and other countries make a pilgrimage to Yazd in Iran to worship at the mountain grotto containing the sacred spring dedicated to Pir-e Sabz. Here worshipers pray for fertile rains and celebrate the greenery of nature and the renewal of life. As Babayan states, "Khijar is related to the Zoroastrian water goddess Anahita, and some of her former sanctuaries in Iran were dedicated to her (Pir-e Sabz)".

Al-Khizr and Alexander the Great in front of the Fountain of Life Various accounts associate al-Khizr with the figure of Dhu al-Qarnayn, identified as either Cyrus the Great or the Himyarite king aʿb. In one version, al-Khizr Khizr and Dhul-Qarnain cross the land of darkness to find the water of life. Dhul-Qarnayn gets lost looking for the spring but Al-Khiyar finds it and gains eternal life. According to Wahhab ibn Munabih, quoted by Ibn Hisham, the king was given the title of Dhu al-Qarnayn by al-Khizr after meeting him in Jerusalem. There are also several versions of the Alexander Romance in which al-Khizr is portrayed as a servant of Alexander the Great. In the Iskandarnama by an unknown author, al-Khizr is told by Dhul-Qarnan to lead him and his forces to the waters of life. Al-Khizr agrees, and eventually stumbles upon the waters of life on his own.

Khizr's role is expanded in the 13th-century Surat al-Iskandar, where he remains Alexander's companion throughout. Some scholars suggest that al-Khizr is also depicted as the Green Knight in the Arthurian tale Sir Gawain and the Green Knight. In the story, the Green Knight tempts Sir Gawain's trust three times. The character of al-Khizr may have entered European literature through the mixing of cultures during the Crusades. It is also possible that the story derives from an Irish myth that predates the Crusades, in which Cu Chulainn and two other heroes compete for the Cuirdmir, the chosen portion given to champions at feasts;

Ultimately, Cú Chulainn is the only one willing to let a giant – actually a king who has magically disguised himself – behead him as per their agreement. In some parts of India, Al-Khizr is also known as Khwaja Khizr, a river of wells and rivers. He is mentioned in the Sikandar-nama as a saint who presides over the well of immortality, and is revered by both Hindus and Muslims. He is sometimes depicted as an old man dressed in green, and is believed to be riding a fish. His main temple is on an island in the Indus River in Punjab, Pakistan by Bhaker. In The Unreasoning Mask by noted science fiction author Philip Jose Farmer, while Al-Buraq captains the Ramstan, a rare model spaceship that can travel instantaneously between two points Able to travel, he attempts to stop an unknown creature that is destroying intelligent life across planets. universe, he is haunted by repeating visions of meeting Al-Kheir.

The story of Al-Khizr in the Holy Qur'an

[Quran Chapter 18]

65. Then they came upon a servant of Ours, whom We had blessed with mercy from Us, and had taught him knowledge from Our Own.

66. Moses said to him, "May I follow you, so that you may teach me some of the guidance you were taught?"

67. He said, "You will not be able to endure with me.

68. And how will you endure what you have no knowledge of?"

69. He said, "You will find me, Allah willing, patient; and I will not disobey you in any order of yours."

70. He said, "If you follow me, do not ask me about anything, until I myself make mention of it to you."

71. So they set out. Until, when they had boarded the boat, he holed it. He said, "Did you hole it, to drown its passengers? You have done something awful."

72. He said, "Did I not tell you that you will not be able to endure with me?"

73. He said, "Do not rebuke me for forgetting, and do not make my course difficult for me."

74. Then they set out. Until, when they encountered a boy, he killed him. He said, "Did you kill a pure soul, who killed no one? You have done something terrible."

75. He said, "Did I not tell you that you will not be able to endure with me?"

76. He said, "If I ask you about anything after this, then do not keep company with me. You have received excuses from me."

77. So they set out. Until, when they reached the people of a town, they asked them for food, but they refused to offer them hospitality. There they found a wall about to collapse, and he repaired it. He said, "If you wanted, you could have obtained a payment for it."

78. He said, "This is the parting between you and me. I will tell you the interpretation of what you were unable to endure.

79. As for the boat, it belonged to paupers working at sea. I wanted to damage it because there was a king coming after them seizing every boat by force.

80. As for the boy, his parents were believers, and we feared he would overwhelm them with oppression and disbelief.

81. So we wanted their Lord to replace him with someone better in purity, and closer to mercy.

82. And as for the wall, it belonged to two orphaned boys in the town. Beneath it was a treasure that belonged to them. Their father was a righteous man. Your Lord wanted them to reach their maturity, and then extract their treasure—as a mercy from your Lord. I did not do it of my own accord. This is the interpretation of what you were unable to endure."

In the Quran 18:65–82,

Moses meets the Servant of God, referred to in the Quran as "one of our slaves whom We had granted mercy from Us and whom We had taught knowledge from Ourselves".[31] Muslim scholars identify him as Khiḍr, although he is not explicitly named in the Quran and there is no reference to him being immortal or being especially associated with esoteric knowledge or fertility.[32] These associations come in later scholarship on al-Khiḍr.[33]

The Quran states that they meet at the junction of two seas, where a fish that Moses and his servant had intended to eat has escaped. Moses asks for permission to accompany the Servant of God so Moses can learn "right knowledge of what [he has] been taught".[34] The Servant informs him that "surely you [Moses] cannot have patience with me. And how canst thou have patience about things about which thy understanding is not complete?"[35] Moses promises to be patient and obey him unquestioningly, and they set out together. After they board a ship, the Servant of God damages the vessel. Forgetting his oath, Moses says, "Have you made a hole in it to drown its inmates? Certainly you have done a grievous thing." The Servant reminds Moses of his warning, "Did I not say that you will not be able to have patience with me?" and Moses pleads not to be rebuked.

Next, the Servant of God kills a young man. Moses again cries out in astonishment and dismay, and again the Servant reminds Moses of his warning, and Moses promises that he will not violate his oath again, and that if he does he will excuse himself from the Servant's presence. They then proceed to a town where they are denied hospitality. This time, instead of harming anyone or anything, the Servant of God restores a decrepit wall in the village. Yet again Moses is amazed and violates his oath for the third and last time, asking why the Servant did not at least exact "some recompense for it."

The Servant of God replies, "This shall be separation between me and you; now I will inform you of the significance of that with which you could not have patience. Many acts which seem to be evil, malicious or somber, actually are merciful. The boat was damaged to prevent its owners from falling into the hands of a king who seized every boat by force. And as for the boy, his parents were believers and we feared lest he should make disobedience and ingratitude to come upon them. God will replace the child with one better in purity, affection and obedience. As for the restored wall, the Servant explained that underneath the wall was a treasure belonging to two helpless orphans whose father was a righteous man. As God's envoy, the Servant restored the wall , showing God's kindness by rewarding the piety of the orphans' father, and so that when the wall becomes weak again and collapses, the orphans will be older and stronger and will take the treasure that belongs to them

Tafsir

ALA-MAUDUDI

The name of this servant has been stated to be Khidr in all the authentic books of traditions. Thus there is no reason why it should be considered at all that his name was Elijah, as some people have asserted under the influence of the Israelite traditions. Their assertion is incorrect not only because it contradicts the assertion of the Prophet (peace be upon him) but it is also absurd because Prophet Elijah (peace be upon him) was born several hundred years after Prophet Moses (peace be upon him). Though the Quran does not mention the name of the attendant of Prophet Moses (peace be upon him), according to some traditions he was Joshua, the son of Nun, who succeeded him.

Tafseer – Daawatul Quran

As far as the general commentators are concerned, they consider this servant of God to be a prophet. However, some think that he was an angel. His argument is not supported by the words of the verse: To whom We had mercy from Our side, because nowhere in the Qur'an is such a statement made about any angel that he was blessed or was merciful by . God . And angels are appointed to carry out divine orders relating to creation or effecting changes. Therefore, the statement of being blessed with mercy may not fit an angel but is quite fitting for a prophet.

Allah had blessed the prophets with different distinctions: Prophet Moses had the honor of conversing with God, while Prophet Isa was given the miracle of reviving the dead; Prophet Yusuf was given the knowledge of interpretation or understanding of dreams, while Prophet Sulaiman Was awarded the gift of understanding the language of birds. Similarly Prophet Khidr was blessed with the talent to understand the mysteries of external events and circumstances, which developed in him an extraordinary ability to understand the significance of worldly events. Prophet Musa was a very high ranking prophet who wanted to benefit from this special knowledge of Prophet Khidr, and for that purpose he made this journey.

Prophet Khidr used to take appropriate steps regarding the secrets of creation that were revealed to him by Allah, but since Prophet Musa was not aware of the realities behind the secrets, it was appropriate to think about the steps taken by Prophet Khidr as wrong; And man reaches a decision only after seeing the outer form of things. Therefore, Prophet Khidr's misapprehension was correct that Prophet Musa would not be able to tolerate the extraordinary things he would do.

This was the test of Prophet Moses in terms of gaining knowledge. The strict condition of not questioning him was imposed by Prophet Khidr so that Prophet Musa would clearly realize the true position regarding the edge of his knowledge and the nature of his work.

Reference – Tafseer – Daawatul Quran

Tafsir - Ibn kasir
This was Al-Khidr, peace be upon him, as is indicated by the authentic Hadiths narrated from the Messenger of Allah.
Al-Bukhari recorded that Sa`id bin Jubayr said,

I said to Ibn Abbas:`Nawf Al-Bikali claims that Musa, the companion of Al-Khidr was not the Musa of the Children of Israel.

Ibn `Abbas said, `The enemy of Allah has told a lie.

Ubayy bin Ka`b narrated that he heard the Messenger of Allah say, Musa got up to deliver a speech before the Children of Israel and he was asked, Who is the most learned person among the people?

Musa replied, I am.

Allah rebuked him because he did not refer the knowledge to Allah.

So Allah revealed to him:At the junction of the two seas there is a servant of Ours who is more learned than you.

Musa asked, O my Lord, how can I meet him?

Allah said, Take a fish and put it in a vessel and then set out, and where you lose the fish, you will find him.

So Musa took a fish, put it in a vessel and set out, along with his boy-servant Yusha` bin Nun, peace be upon him, till they reached a rock (on which) they both lay down their heads and slept. The fish moved vigorously in the vessel and got out of it and fell into the sea and there it took its way through the sea (straight) as in a tunnel.

Allah stopped the flow of water on both sides of the way created by the fish, and so that way was like a tunnel.

When Musa got up, his companion forgot to tell him about the fish, and so they carried on their journey during the rest of the day and the whole night.

The next morning Musa said to his boy-servant,

Bring us our morning meal; truly, we have suffered much fatigue in this, our journey.

Musa did not get tired till he had passed the place that Allah had ordered him to look for. His boy-servant then said to him,
Do you remember when we betook ourselves to the rock I indeed forgot the fish; none but Shaytan made me forget to remember it. It took its course into the sea in a strange way.

There was a tunnel for the fish and Musa and his boy-servant were amazed. Musa said,

ذَلِكَ مَا كُنَّا نَبْغِ فَارْتَدَّا عَلَى ءَاثَارِهِمَا قَصَصًا

That is what we have been seeking.So they went back retracing their footsteps.

So they went back retracing their steps until they reached the rock. There they found a man covered with a garment.

Musa greeted him.

Al-Khidr said, Is there such a greeting in your land!

Musa said, I am Musa.

He said, Are you the Musa of the Children of Israel?

Musa said, Yes,and added, I have come to you so that you may teach me something of that knowledge which you have been taught.

قَالَ إِنَّكَ لَن تَسْتَطِيعَ مَعِيَ صَبْراً

Al-Khidr said, You will not be able to have patience with me.

O Musa! I have some of Allahs knowledge which He has bestowed upon me but you do not know it; and you too, have some of Allahs knowledge which He has bestowed upon you, but I do not know it.

Musa said,

سَتَجِدُنِى إِن شَاءَ اللَّهُ صَابِرًا وَلَا أَعْصِى لَكَ أَمْراً

If Allah wills, you will find me patient, and I will not disobey you in aught.

Al-Khidr said to him,

فَإِنِ اتَّبَعْتَنِى فَلَ تَسْأَلْنِى عَن شَىءٍ حَتَّى أُحْدِثَ لَكَ مِنْهُ ذِكْراً

Then, if you follow me, ask me not about anything till I myself mention it to you.

So they set out walking along the shore, until a boat passed by and they asked the crew to let them go on board.

The crew recognized Al-Khidr and allowed them to go on board free of charge.

When they went on board, suddenly Musa saw that Al-Khidr had pulled out one of the planks of the ship with an adz.

Musa said to him, These people gave us a free ride, yet you have broken their boat so that its people will drown!

Verily, you have done a terrible thing!

قَالَ أَلَمْ أَقُلْ إِنَّكَ لَن تَسْتَطِيعَ مَعِىَ صَبْراً

Al-Khidr said, Did I not tell you, that you would not be able to have patience with me!

قَالَ لَا تُوَاخِذْنِى بِمَا نَسِيتُ وَلَا تُرْهِقْنِى مِنْ أَمْرِى عُسْراً

Musa said, Call me not to account for what I forgot and be not hard upon me for my affair (with you).

The Messenger of Allah said,

In the first instance, Musa asked Al-Khidr because he had forgotten his promise.

Then a bird came and sat on the edge of the boat, dipping its beak once or twice in the sea. Al-Khidr said to Musa, My knowledge and your knowledge, in comparison to Allahs knowledge, is like what this bird has taken out of the sea.

Then they both disembarked from the boat, and while they were walking on the shore, Al-Khidr saw a boy playing with other boys.

Al-Khidr took hold of the boys head and pulled it off with his hands, killing him.

Musa said to him,

فَانْطَلَقَا حَتَّى إِذَا لَقِيَا غُلَمًا فَقَتَلَهُ قَالَ أَقَتَلْتَ نَفْسًا زَكِيَّةً بِغَيْرِ نَفْسٍ لَّقَدْ جِئْتَ شَيْئاً نُّكْراً

Have you killed an innocent person who had killed none! Verily, you have committed a thing Nukr!

قَالَ أَلَمْ أَقُلْ لَّكَ إِنَّكَ لَن تَسْتَطِيعَ مَعِىَ صَبْراً

He said, Did I not tell you that you would not be able to have patience with me

(The narrator) said, "The second blame was stronger than the first one".

Musa said, "If I ask you anything after this, keep me not in your company; you have received an excuse from me." Then they both proceeded until they came to the people of a town. They asked them for food but they refused to entertain them. (Then) they found there a wall on the point of falling down.

(Al-Khidr) set it up straight with his own hands.

Musa said, "We came to these people, but they neither fed us nor received us as guests. If you had wished, surely, you could have taken wages for it!"

قَالَ هَـذَا فِرَاقُ بَيْنِى وَبَيْنِكَ سَأُنَبِّئُكَ بِتَأْوِيلِ مَا لَمْ تَسْتَطِع عَّلَيْهِ صَبْراً

(Al-Khidr) said:"This is the parting between you and I. I will tell you the interpretation of (those) things over which you were unable to be patient."

The Messenger of Allah said:

وَدِدْنَا أَنَّ مُوسَى كَانَ صَبَرَ حَتَّى يَقُصَّ اللهُ عَلَيْنَا مِنْ خَبَرِهِمَا

We wish that Musa was patient so that Allah would have told us more about both of them.

Sa'id bin Jubayr said:

"Ibn Abbas used to recite (Ayah no. 79),

وَكَانَ أَمَامَهُمْ مَلِكٌ يَأْخُذُ كُلَّ سَفِينَةٍ صَالَحَةٍ غَضْبًا

There was a king before them who seized every good-conditioned ship by force.

and (Ayah no 80)

وَأَمَّا الْغُلَامُ فَكَانَ كَافِرًا وَكَانَ أَبَوَاهُ مُؤْمِنَيْنِ

As for the boy, he was a disbeliever and his parents were believers.

Then (in another narration) Al-Bukhari recorded a similar account which says:
then Musa set out and with him was his boy-servant Yusha` bin Nun, and they had the fish with them. When they reached the rock, they camped there, and Musa lay down his head and slept. At the base of the rock there was a spring called Al-Hayat; its water never touched a thing but it brought it to life. Some of its water touched the fish, so it began to move and jumped out of the vessel and into the sea. When he woke up, Musa said to his boy-servant:

Bring us our morning meal.

Then he quoted the rest of the Hadith.

Then a bird came and perched on the edge of the ship, and dipped its beak in the sea, and Al-Khidr said to Musa,

"My knowledge and your knowledge and the knowledge of all of creation, in comparison to the knowledge of Allah, is like what this bird has taken from the sea."

Tafsir/ Abu Bakr Al-Jazairi (b. 1921 AD)

Abu Bakr al-Jazaeri

Abu Bakr Jabir bin Musa bin Abdul Qadir ibn Jaber, better known as Abu Bakr al-Jazairi (1921 – 15 August 2018), was an Algerian Sunni Islamic scholar.

Biography– Al-Jazairi was born in 1921 in the village of Lioua, close to Tolga, which is located today in the state of Biskra Province in Algeria. In his hometown grew up and received his primary education, and began to memorize the Quran and some Almtun language and jurisprudence of Maliki, and then moved to the city of

Biskra, where started to teach in a private school. Then he traveled with his family to Medina, and in the Prophet's Mosque resumed his education way to sit to the circles of scholars and sheikhs where he got permission from the Presidency of the judiciary in Mecca to teach in the Prophet's Mosque. He worked as a teacher in some schools of the Ministry of Education and in Dar Al Hadith in Madinah. When the Islamic University of Madinah opened its doors in 1961, he was one of its first teachers and teachers, and remained there until he retired in 1987.

He was under the teachings of sheiks as Naim Al-Nuaimi, Issa Mutawqi and Tayeb Al-Aqbi in Algeria, and Omar Berry and Mohammed Al-Hafiz in Medina. One of his disciples was Saleh Al Maghamsi.

Abu Bakr al-Jazairi was widely known for teaching in the Prophet's Mosque for 50 years and in Islamic University of Medina, which earned his lessons and books great momentum. His book The Platform of the Muslim is one of his most widely accepted works in the Arab countries. He refused to compliment by the financial sector and warned against riba in his book to the prayers. He wrote a book in particular his advice to every Shiite.

He died in Medina on Wednesday 15 August 2018 at the age of 97.

Before leaving Algeria he was involved in politics and participated in the Bayan party. He also participated in the establishment of the Unionist Youth Movement, a unitary Islamic movement, later known for his opposition to the Houari Boumédiène regime. After settling in Saudi Arabia, he focused on the scientific side without forgetting to talk about ideological and politics. He declared his opposition to atoning the Muslim rulers and exiting them. He believed that all this was achieved only in the light of the Quran and Sunnah. In the jihad, he was against the Soviet occupation of Afghanistan in the 1980s.

Interpretation of Aasr al-Tafsir of the words of the Most High/Abu Bakr al-Jaza'iri (d. 1921 AD)

words explanation:
And when Moses said to his girl: That is, I remember when Moses bin Imran, the Prophet of the Children of Israel, said to his girl, Joshua bin Nun bin Ephraim bin Joseph, peace be upon him.

Bahrain Complex: That is, where the two seas met, the Persian Sea and the Roman Sea.

Era: eras of time, which is eighty years, and the plural is eras.

His path in the sea is a swarm: that is, his path in the sea is a swarm, that is, a path like a tunnel.

When they passed: that is, the place where the rock was, and from there, the whale made its way into the sea as a swarm.

There is a wonder in the sea: that is, the wonder of Moses, as he was amazed at the whale being revived and taking a path in the sea like a tunnel in the mountain.

Stories: that is, they trace their footprints.

One of our servants: Al-Khidr, peace be upon him.

From what I have learned is guidance: that is, what is guidance to the truth and evidence of guidance.

Unless you have any knowledge: that is, knowledge.

I will not disobey your command: that is, I will do what you command me to do, even if it does not agree with my desires.
Meaning of the verses:
This is the story of Moses and Al-Khidr, peace be upon them, and it confirms and confirms the prophecy of Muhammad, may God bless

him and grant him peace. Because such stories are true, it is not possible for anyone to tell them unless they receive revelation from God Almighty. The Almighty said: {And when Moses said} meaning, "Remember, O our Messenger, as evidence of our oneness, our meeting, and your prophecy." When Moses bin Imran, our Prophet, said to the children of Israel to his servant, Joshua bin Nun, {I will not depart} that is, I will walk {until I reach the gathering of the two seas} where my Lord guided me to meet a servant there from among His servants who is more knowledgeable than me so that I may learn from him knowledge that I will add to my knowledge, {or I will go on for a while. } That is, I will continue my journey for a long time until I find this good servant to learn about him. God Almighty says: {And when they reached it, they gathered together} meaning between the two seas, which are the Sea of Rum and the Persian Sea, at Bab al-Mandab, where the Red Sea and the Indian Sea met. Or the White Sea and the Atlantic Sea near Tangier, and God knows which one he wanted. His saying, "They forgot their whale," meaning the boy forgot the whale, since he was the one who was carrying him, but forgetfulness was attributed to them according to what is known from the Arabic language, and this whale was made by God Almighty as a sign to Moses of the presence of Al-Khidr, where the whale was missing, since the story is as in Al-Bukhari.

Al-Khizr's name in various texts -

al-Kidr in Arabic, al-Qadr, al-Qadr, al-Kedr in the Holy Qur'an Khabira, Kabiran, Khabiran; Kabir in the holy Fazle Amal, Hudra in the Yiddish language of the Jews, Kisir in Persian and Hizir in Turkic South India and Sri Lanka, Qatar, Khadar, Khadir, Khizar, Khidr, Al Khidr in Hindi, Kabir, Kabira, Holy Vedas and KavirDev in Sanskrit, KavirDev Kabir in the Holy Orthodox Juish Bible Kabir in the Holy Guru Granth Sahib Eliyah in the Middle East and Greece, Elias in the states of the Balkan Peninsula region of South Eastern Europe Green jor.

In Hadith

Al-Khiḍr is a figure in Islamic tradition who is believed to have the appearance of a young adult but with a long, white beard. According to some authors, al-Khiḍr is Xerxes, a 6th-century Sasanian prince who disappeared after finding the fountain of life and sought to live his remaining life in service of God. There are several reported proofs of the life of al-Khiḍr, including one where Muhammad is said to have stated that the prophet Elijah and al-Khiḍr meet every year and spend the month of Ramadan in Jerusalem. Another report states that a man seen walking with Umar II was actually al-Khiḍr. It is also narrated that Al-Khiḍr met with Ali by the Kaaba. It is also told that during the time when the false Messiah appears, a believer will challenge him, who will be sliced into two pieces and rejoined, making it appear that he caused him to die and be resurrected, and this person will be al-Khiḍr.

Muhammad al-Bukhari reports that al-Khiḍr got his name after he was present over the surface of some ground that became green as a result of his presence there. There are reports from al-Bayhaqi that al-Khiḍr was present at the funeral of Muhammad and was recognized only by Ali from amongst the rest of the companions, and where he came to show his grief and sadness at the death of Muhammad. Al-Khiḍr's appearance at Muhammad's funeral is related as follows: A powerful-looking, fine-featured, handsome man with a white beard came leaping over the backs of the people till he reached where the sacred body lay. Weeping bitterly, he turned toward the Companions and paid his condolences. Ali said that he was Khiḍr.

Ja'far al-Sadiq narrates in Kitab al-Kafi that after entering the sacred Mosque in Mecca, Ali, Hasan ibn Ali, and Husayn ibn Ali were visited by a good looking, well dressed man who asked them a series of questions. Hasan answered the questions and upon this, the man testified to the prophet-hood of Muhammad followed by testifying that Ali and his Ahl al-Bayt are the successors and heir to his message. Ali asked Hasan to track the whereabouts of the visitor, but when he could not, Ali revealed the identity of the man to be Khidr.

The Islamic scholar Said Nursî believed that Khidr, a figure in Islamic tradition, is alive and at the second degree of life. Some religious scholars have doubts about this belief. He said al-Khidr and Elijah were free and able to be present in multiple places at the same time. They do not have to eat or drink and are not restricted by human needs. There is a level of sainthood called "the degree of Khidr" where a person receives instruction from Khidr and meets with him. However, sometimes the person at this level is mistaken for Khidr himself.

Al-Khidr (romanized as al-Khadir, Khader, Khidr, Hidra, Khizr, Kejar, Kathir, Khazar, Khader, Kheder, Khizir, Khizar, Khilar) is a figure not mentioned by name in the Quran. He is described in Surah al-Kahf, as a righteous servant of God possessing great wisdom or mystic knowledge. In various Islamic and non-Islamic traditions, Khidr is described as an angel, prophet or wali, who protects the sea, teaches secret knowledge and aids people in distress. He figures prominently as the mentor of the Islamic saint Ibn Arabi. The image of al-Khidr has over time been syncretized with a number of other figures, including Duraosha and Sorush in Iran, Sargis the General and Saint George in Asia Minor and the Levant, Samael (divine prosecutor) in Judaism, Elijah among the Druze, John the Baptist in Armenia, and Jhulelal in Sindh and Punjab in South Asia, where he is remembered on the holiday of Hidirelez.

Al-Khidr

Al-Khadir

Al-Khidr shown riding on a fish, as depicted in a mid-17th century

Although the Quran does not mention him by name, Islamic scholars have named him as the person mentioned in Quran 18:65-82, as a servant of God who is given "knowledge" and who accompanies the prophet Moses (Moses) and questions him about several improper or unjust actions he (al-Khidr) has committed (sinking a ship, killing a young man, repaying inhumanity by repairing a wall). At the end of the story Khidr explains circumstances unknown to Moses that made each action just and proper.

Many mystics and some scholars who give credence to the narration of Abu Ishaq's hadith about Khidr's meeting with the Dajjal (a false messiah character in Islamic eschatology) believe that Khidr is still alive, while there are other, contradictory, more credible narrations and verses that account for the legend.

Islamic view

Muhammad ibn Jarir al-Tabari, a Persian scholar, historian and interpreter of the Quran in Sunni Islam, writes about Khidr in a chapter of his History of the Prophets called "The Story of al-Khidr and His History; and the History of Moses and His Servant Joshua." Al-Tabari describes several versions of the traditional story surrounding al-Khidr. At the beginning of the chapter, al-Tabari explains that in some variations, al-Khidr is a contemporary of the mythical Persian king Afridun, who was a contemporary of Abraham, and lived before the days of Moses. Al-Khidr was also appointed as the vanguard of King Dhul-Qarnayn the Elder, who is identified in this version as King Afridun. In this specific version, al-Khidr comes across the River of Life and, unaware of its virtues, drinks from it and becomes immortal. Al-Tabari also reports that al-Khidr is said to be the son of a man who believed in Abraham, and had accompanied Abraham on the migration when the latter left Babylon.

Al-Khidr is also commonly associated with Elijah, even considered his equal, and al-Tabari makes a distinction in the next account in which al-Khidr is Persian and Elijah is an Israelite. According to this version of al-Khidr's story, al-Khidr and Elijah meet every year during the annual festival season.

Al-Tabari believes that al-Khidr lived in the time of Afridun, before Moses, rather than the time he traveled as a companion of Abraham and drank the water of life. He does not explicitly state why he has this preference, but rather it seems that he prefers the chain of sources (isnad) of the former story rather than that of the latter.

The various versions in al-Tabari's history more or less parallel each other and the details described in the Quran. However, in the stories told by al-Tabari, Moses claims to be the most knowledgeable man on earth, and God corrects him by telling him to look for al-Khidr. Moses is told to fetch salted fish, and when he finds the fish missing, he seeks out al-Khidr. Moses sets out on a journey with a traveling companion, and when they reach a certain rock, the fish comes to life, jumps into the water, and swims away. This is the point where Moses and his companion meet al-Khidr. Al-Tabari also gives information on the origin of al-Khidr's name. He cites a saying of Muhammad that al-Khidr ("the green" or "the green") was so named because he sat on a white fur and it shone green with him.

In Shia Islam

Some Shia Muslims believe that al-Khidr accompanied Muhammad al-Mahdi to meet Sheikh Hasan ibn Muthalih Jamkarani on 22 February 984 AD (17 Ramadan 373 AH) and instructed him to build the Jamkaran Mosque on the site of their meeting. The site, located six kilometres east of Qom, Iran, has been a pilgrimage site for Shias for some time.

In Ismailism, al-Khidr is regarded as one of the 'permanent Imams'; that is, those who have guided people throughout history.

In Sufi thought

In the Sufi tradition, al-Khidr holds a revered position as one who receives light directly from God without any human mediation. He is believed to be alive and many respected figures, sheikhs and prominent leaders of the Sufi community claim to have encountered him in person. Examples of those who make such a claim are Abdul-Qadir Gilani, al-Nawawi, Ibn Arabi, Sidi Abdul Aziz ad-Dabbagh and Ahmad ibn Idris al-Fasi. Ibn Ata Allah's Lata'if al-minan (1:84–98) states that there is a consensus among Sufis that al-Khidr is alive.There are also a number of Sufi orders that claim their origin from al-Khidr or that al-Khidr is part of their spiritual chain, including the Naqshbandi Haqqani Sufi orders, the Muhammadiyah, the Idrisiya, and the Senussi. He is the hidden initiator for Uwaysi Sufis, who enter the mystical path without receiving initiation from a living master, instead following the guiding light of earlier masters or, in their belief system, by receiving initiation from al-Khidr. Thus al-Khidr himself had become a symbol of access to the divine mystery (ghayb), and in the writings of Abd al-Karim al-Jili, al-Khidr rules over the 'invisible ones' (rijalu'l-ghayb). Al-Khidr is also called 'the Abdal' ('those who act in turn') in classical Sufism. In the Sufi hierarchy, "Abdal" is a mystical rank, of which al-Khidr is the spiritual head.

The Sri Lankan Sufi Bawa Muhyiddin also gives a unique account of al-Khidr. Al-Khidr had long been in search of God, until God in His mercy sent the Archangel Gabriel to guide him. Gabriel appears to al-Khidr as a wise human sage, and al-Khidr accepts him as his teacher. Gabriel teaches al-Khidr in the same way that al-Khidr later taught Moses in the Quran, by teaching by carrying out actions that appear to be unjust. Al-Khidr repeatedly breaks his oath not to speak against Gabriel's actions, and is still unaware that the human teacher is in fact Gabriel. Gabriel then explains his actions, and shows al-Khidr his true angelic form. Al-Khidr identifies him as the Archangel Gabriel, and then Gabriel grants al-Khidr a spiritual title by calling him Hayat Nabi, i.e., Eternal Life Prophet. The French scholar of Sufism Henri Corbin interprets al-Khidr as the mystical prophet, the eternal wanderer. Al-Khidr's task as 'person-archetype' is to reveal himself to each disciple, to lead each disciple to his own divine vision, because that divine vision corresponds to his own 'inner paradise', his own nature of being, his eternal personality. Accordingly, al-Khidr is Moses' spiritual guide, initiating Moses into the divine sciences, and revealing to him secret mystical truths. The Moroccan Sufi Abdul Aziz ad-Dabbagh describes al-Khidr as acting under the guidance of divine revelation (wahi), as other saints do, without the need for a prophet. Compared to other saints, God gave al-Khidr the powers and knowledge of the highest-ranking saint (al-Gawth), such as the power of free disposal reaching far beyond the Arsh and keeping in memory all God-sent scriptures.

In Ahmadiyya

Ahmadiyya interpretations of the Quran regard the account of Moses meeting the "Servant of God" as a symbolic representation of Muhammad. Ahmadis hold that the Quranic passage of Moses' meeting with the "Servant of God" is, contextually, closely linked to the subject matter of Surah al Kahf in which their story is cited. According to Ahmadiyya commentaries, Moses' visit and his meeting with the "Servant of God" was a visionary experience similar to Muhammad's Miraj (ascension), which Moses had wished to see and was shown to him in this vision. The nature of the dialogue between Moses and the "Servant of God" and the relationship between them are seen as indicative of the personal characteristics of Moses and Muhammad as well as of their respective followers and the entire Quranic narrative is understood as an allegory of Muhammad's spiritual superiority over Moses and the supersession of the Jewish order by the Islamic order.

In the Druze faith

Two saints in the Druze religion are identified as "El-Khidr": Saint George (left) and Saint Elijah (right)

The Druze worship Elijah and he is considered a central figure in Druzism. The Druze regard the cave of Elijah as sacred, and they identify Elijah as "El-Khidr", the green-robed prophet who symbolizes water and life, a miracle worker who heals the sick. The Druze generally view El Khidr, John the Baptist, and Saint George as successive reincarnations of the same soul, in keeping with their beliefs in these concepts.

Saint George is described as a prophetic figure in Druze sources; and in some sources he is identified with Elijah (Mar Elias), and in others as Al-Khidr. The Druze version of the story of Al-Khidr was syncretized with the story of Saint George and the Dragon.

Due to Christian influence on the Druze faith, two Christian saints became favorite revered figures of the Druze: Saint George and Saint Elijah. Thus, all villages inhabited by Druze and Christians in central Mount Lebanon have a Christian church or Druze maqam dedicated to one of them. According to scholar Ray Jabre Mouawad the Druze admired the two saints for their bravery: Saint George because he confronted the dragon and Saint Elijah because he competed with and conquered the pagan priests of Baal. In both cases the explanation provided by Christians is that the Druze were attracted to warrior saints who resembled their own militarized society.

Verve for Saint George, often identified with al-Khidr, is deeply integrated into various aspects of Druze culture and religious practices. He is seen as the patron of the Druze community and a symbol of their enduring faith and resilience. Additionally, Saint George is regarded in Druze tradition as a protector and healer. The story of Saint George slaying the dragon is interpreted allegorically, representing the victory of good over evil and protecting believers from harm.

In Zoroastrianism

In Iran there are several figures who were replaced by Khidr in the process of Islamization. One of them is paradoxically a female figure, Anahita. The most popular temple in Yazd is dedicated to Anahita. For pilgrims to Yazd, among Zoroastrians, the most important of the six pirs is the Pir-e Sabz ("Green Temple"). The name of the temple derives from the greenery of the foliage that grows around the sanctuary. It is still a functional temple and the most sacred site for present-day Zoroastrians living in Iran.

Every year from June 14 to 18, thousands of Zoroastrians from Iran, India and other countries make a pilgrimage to Yazd, Iran to worship in a mountain cave containing a sacred spring dedicated to Pir-e Sabz. Here the faithful pray for fertile rains and celebrate the greening of nature and the renewal of life.

As Babayan says, "Khizr is related to the Zoroastrian water goddess Anahita, and some of his former sanctuaries in Iran were rededicated to him (Pir-i sabz)".

Theories on the origin

Al-Khidr and Alexander the Great before the Fountain of Life
The source of the Quranic episode of Moses' visit with al-Khidr has been the subject of varying opinions of various scholars. Like some other scholars, Brannon notes that the story does not seem to have any direct Christian or Jewish predecessor. But a very recent study has shown that the Quranic story is full of Jewish symbols, even if we cannot historically identify its possible original form.

In one of the most influential hypotheses on the source of the al-Khidr story, the early twentieth-century Dutch historian Arent Jan Wensink [de] argued that the story was derived from a Jewish legend involving the Talmudic rabbi Joshua ben Levi and the holy prophet Elijah. Like Moses and al-Khidr, Joshua asks to follow Elijah, who agrees on the condition that the former will not question any of his actions. One night, Joshua and Elijah are hosted by a poor man who has only a cow, which Elijah kills. The next day, they are refused hospitality by a rich man, but the Prophet fixes the man's wall without receiving pay. Finally, the two are refused hospitality by people in a wealthy synagogue. When Joshua questions the Prophet, the Prophet explains that he killed the cow as a replacement for the soul of the man's wife, who was to die that day; he fixed the wall because there was treasure beneath it that the rich man could find while fixing it himself; and his prayer was because a land under one ruler is better than a land under many rulers.This Jewish legend is first attested in an Arabic work by the eleventh-century Tunisian Jewish scholar Nissim ben Jacob, some four hundred years after the composition of the Quran. Haim Schwarzbaum [de] argued as early as 1960 that the story appears to be "entirely dependent on the Quranic text", with even the language being more similar to typical Classical Arabic than to Ben Jacob's other stories with clear Talmudic origins. Noting that Ben Jacob's compilation also includes other stories with clear Islamic antecedents, Wheeler also suggests that the Jewish story of Elijah was created under Islamic influence, remarking that its similarities with the story of al-Khidr are more closely linked to the elaborations of later Islamic commentaries rather than to the Quran's concise narrative. For example, in the Jewish story ben Levi deliberately seeks out Elijah, just as God tells Moses to seek out al-Khidr in Islamic commentaries, while the Quran itself never says whether the meeting between Moses and al-Khidr is deliberate or accidental. The close association between Elijah and al-Khidr is also attested for the first time by several early Islamic sources. Ben Jacob may have changed the character of the disciple from Moses to Joshua ben Levi because he was wary of attributing negative qualities to a Jewish prophet and because ben Levi was already a familiar recurring character in Jewish literature.Another early tale similar to the story of Khidr is related to Christianity. A damaged and non-standard thirteenth-century Greek manuscript of the Leimon Pneumatikos, a pious work by the pre-Islamic Byzantine monk John Moschus, includes the conclusion of a narrative involving an angel and a monk, in which the angel tells of some peculiar actions he had presumably committed earlier, now lost sections of the narrative. The angel had stolen a chalice from a generous host, because he knew that the chalice was stolen and that their host would be unwittingly sinning if he kept it. He had killed the son of another generous host, because he knew that the boy would become a sinner when he reached adulthood, but would go to heaven if he died before he committed his sin. Finally, the angel repaired the wall of a man who had refused them hospitality, because he knew that there was treasure underneath that the man could have found otherwise. The story of the angel and the monk is part of a wider Late Antique Christian tradition of theodicy. French historian Roger Paret points out that the story of Moschus is much more closely related to the Quranic episode than to the Jewish legend; for example, the angel in the Greek story and the "servant of God" in the Quran are both anonymous and vaguely defined, in contrast to the named figures of the Jewish Elijah or Khidr in Islamic interpretation. Islamic theology scholar Gabriel Said Reynolds has regarded the story of Moschus as a possible source for the Quranic narrative.Schwarzbaum has argued that the Quranic narrative originated in a Late Antique context in which Christian theodicy legends involving monks were popular, which equated Christian pneumatics with knowledge received directly from God. Schwarzbaum also speculates on an ultimately Jewish prototype for Khidr, possibly a legend in which Moses becomes a disciple of the future Rabbi Akiva, compiler of the Oral Torah. While agreeing that the Quranic story "combines disparate elements from motifs present in late antiquity", Wheeler rejects Schwarzbaum's connection between Rabbi Akiva and Khidr.

In the Quranic story that just precedes Moses' encounter with Khidr, a fish that Moses and his servant had intended to eat escapes into the sea, and when the Prophet returns to the spot where the fish escaped, he encounters Khidr. The fish episode is generally taken to be derived from an episode in the Alexander Romance of Late Antiquity The story is believed to be the one in which Alexander's cook discovers the Fountain of Life while washing a dead fish in it, which then comes to life and escapes. The Alexander Romance is partly derived from the ancient Epic of Gilgamesh, meaning that the Quranic narrative is ultimately related to the story of Gilgamesh.Some scholars, including Wensink, have argued that certain elements of the story of Moses and Khidr appear to be influenced by the Epic of Gilgamesh. In this line of analysis, Khidr is considered the Islamic counterpart of Utnapishtim, the immortal sage of Mesopotamian mythology with esoteric knowledge from the gods, whom Gilgamesh unsuccessfully consults to obtain immortality. Khidr is similar to Utnapishtim in that they are both considered immortal – although the former's immortality is only mentioned in later Islamic sources, not in the Quran, and this immortality only means extremely long life since in Islam everyone except God will eventually die – and in that Moses encounters Khidr at the "meeting place of the two waters"

Another hypothesis on Khidr's origin compares him to the Ugaritic god Kothar-wa-Khasis. The two characters have some surprisingly common features. For example, Kothar and Khidr possess wisdom and esoteric knowledge. Both figures are involved in killing a dragon. Kothar helps Baal kill Yam-Nahar by making weapons for him. Khidr helps Sufis or wali's such as Sari Saltik struggle with the dragon. Both are also known as "sailor" figures who are symbolically connected to the sea, lakes and rivers. Khidr often has some characteristics of a sailor, even in cultural regions not directly connected to the sea, such as mountainous Dersim. However, according to a recent (2019) view, although Khidr has some common features derived from the mythological figure of Elijah transferred from Kothar and Hasis, he is actually a syncretized form of Enoch and Elijah. Because the Quranic story about Khidr which is mentioned anonymously in Surat al-Kahf is basically an Enochian version of the Elijah story. A minor theory suggested that al-Khidr is another name for the Tamil god Murugan as some say their origins are similar to each other, but this theory appears to be unproven.

Comparative mythology

Various accounts associate al-Khidr with Dhu al-Qarnayn, who is commonly identified as Alexander the Great, although a number of Islamic scholars have rejected this claim because Alexander the Great was a polytheist. In one version, al-Khidr and Dhul-Qarnayn cross the land of darkness to find the Water of Life. Dhul-Qarnayn gets lost looking for the spring but al-Khidr finds it and gains eternal life. According to Wahb ibn Munabbih, quoted by Ibn Hisham, Dhu al-Qarnayn was given the title of Raja Sahab by al-Khidr after meeting him in Jerusalem. There are also several versions of the Alexander romance. In the Eskandarnama by an anonymous author, al-Khidr is asked by Dhul-Qarnayn to lead him and his armies to the Water of Life. Al-Khidr agrees, and eventually stumbles upon the Water of Life on his own. Khidr's role is expanded in the 13th-century Sīrat al-Iskandār, where he is Alexander's companion throughout.

Some scholars suggest that al-Khidr is also represented as the Green Knight in the Arthurian tale Sir Gawain and the Green Knight. In the tale, the Green Knight tempts Sir Gawain's confidence three times. The character of al-Khidr may have come into European literature through the mixing of cultures during the Crusades. It is also possible that the tale derives from an Irish myth predating the

Crusades in which Cú Chulainn and two other heroes compete for the curadmír, a select portion awarded to champions at feasts; ultimately, Cú Chulainn is the only one willing to let a giant – in fact a king who has magically disguised himself – cut off his head in accordance with their agreement.In parts of India, al-Khidr is also known as Khawaja Khidr, the river spirit of wells and springs. He is mentioned in the Sikander-Nama as the saint presiding over the Well of Immortality, and is revered by both Hindus and Muslims. He is sometimes depicted as an old man dressed in green, and is believed to ride on a fish. His main temple is on an island in the Indus River near Bhakkar in Punjab, Pakistan.

In the book The Unreasoning Mask by noted science fiction author Philip Jose Farmer, Ramstan, captain of the al-Buraq (a rare model spaceship capable of instantaneous travel between two points), attempts to stop an unknown creature that is destroying intelligent life on planets throughout the universe, and is haunted by recurring visions of meeting al-Khidr.

Is Al-Khidr (PBUH) alive or dead?

Al-Khidr (peace and blessings be upon him) is the righteous servant whom Allah Almighty mentions in the Qur'an in Surat Al-Kahf. Prophet Moses (peace and blessings be upon him) was with Al-Khidr and received many teachings from him. According to the view that is considered the most correct, Al-Khidr is no longer alive. Moreover, he was a prophet according to the predominant view.

The stories of Al-Khidr by righteous people are countless. They claim that he and Ilyas performed Hajj every year and that they recited du'as from him. These stories are well-known and widespread, but the basis of what they say is very weak because most of the stories are narrated from some of those who are considered righteous, or from dreams and hadiths that are related to Anas or others. But they are all da'if or weak and cannot be used to prove anything.

What seems more probable to us, based on the evidence concerning this matter, is that al-Khidr is not alive; rather, he died. This is due to several reasons:

1. The clear meaning of the verse, "And We did not grant immortality to any human being before you; then if you die, will they live forever?" (al-Anbiya: 34)

2. The Prophet (peace and blessings be upon him) is said to have said: "O Allah, if you allow this group of Muslims to be destroyed, you will not be worshiped on earth." (Narrated by Muslim)

3. The Prophet (peace and blessings be upon him) said that a hundred years after the night of which he was speaking, none of the people living on earth would be alive. If al-Khidr had been alive at that time, he would not have survived after the hundred years described. Muslim ibn Hajjaj said that 'Abdullah ibn 'Abdullah ibn 'Umar said, "The Messenger of Allah (peace be upon him) one night in the last days of his life led us to pray 'Isha, then he stood up and said, 'Do you see this night of yours? A hundred years from now none of those who are on earth will survive.' " Ibn 'Umar said, "People did not understand these words of the Messenger of Allah (peace be upon him), and they said that this meant that the Day of Resurrection would come a hundred years later. The Prophet (peace be upon him) said, "'None of those who are on earth will survive' meaning that that generation will pass away."

4. If al-Khidr had been alive at the time of the Prophet (peace and blessings be upon him), al-Khidr would have followed the Prophet, supported him and fought with him because the Prophet was sent to the two races of jinn and humans.

In clarifying whether al-Khidr was a prophet or not, we would like to cite the following: "From the general meaning of the verses of the Qur'an it appears that he was a prophet.

The late prominent Muslim scholar Sheikh Shinqiti (may Allah have mercy on him) said in his commentary on the verse "Then he found one of Our servants on whom We had bestowed mercy from Our side and to whom We had taught wisdom from Our side." (Al-Kahf: 65) But from some verses it can be understood that

the mercy referred to here was the mercy of prophethood The fact that something general is present does not necessarily mean that something more specific is present, as is well known. The indication that the mercy and wisdom which Allah bestowed on His servant al-Khidr came through prophethood and Wahy is the verse "And I did not do them by My own will" (Al-Kahf: 82), that is, I did them by Allah's command; Allah's command is revealed only through Wahy This is because there is no way of knowing Allah's commands and prohibitions except through the Wahy of Allah, particularly with regard to the killing of an apparently innocent soul and damaging a ship by piercing it, since acts of aggression against people's lives and property can only be validated through the Wahy of Allah."

al-Khidr, the Green Man

Idris and al-Khiḍr

Al-Khadir (right) and companion Zul-Qarnain (al-Sikandar) marvel at the sight of a salted fish that comes back to life when touched by the Water of Life

The prophets Elias and Khadir at the fountain of life, late 15th century. Folio from a khamsa (quintet) by Nizami (d. 1209); Timurid period. Opaque watercolor and silver on paper. Herat, Afghanistan, now at The Freer Gallery of Art, Smithsonian Institution

The Biblical Idris is Enoch (Genesis V/23) who lived for 365 years on earth, a healer, teacher, one well versed in sciences and the arts and one whom God took unto himself. The consonants of the word Enoch, mean 'initiated'. Hebrew Hanoch means initiator or opener of the inner eye.

The Koranic Idris is al-Khiḍr who appears in Sura 18/66 (Al Kalf, The Cave), where Moses and his attendant go on a long journey to a point where two rivers met, a point to be seen even though the march would take them ages. According to revelation received by Prophet Mohammad, they meet a personage who is "one of our slaves, unto whom we had taught knowledge peculiar to us" (wa 'allalnnahu min ladunna ilmy). This phrase alone categorically asserts the transmission of theosophia or divine wisdom down the ages, through Divine Guides or Teachers as the word rusted implies in the question Moses asks him: May I follow you on the understanding that you, a rusted teach me, what you have been taught?"

What were the hallmarks of the teachings of the hanifs or illuminati?

Laws of involutionary and evolutionary cycles.
Laws of emanation and manifestation.
Science of the heart-mind (qalb)
Science of Light (hikmat al-ilraq)
The spiritual communion with the hierarchial Beings.
The periodical manifestation of Light called Logos, Christ or Word in Christianity, Buddha in Buddhism. Teerthamkara in Jainism, is termed qutb in Islam. Ali al Hujwiri in Khashf al Mahajab writes of such a hierarchy; "Besides the Qutb or Axis of the Universe, are three called Ifuqaba, four Awtad, seven Abrar". Ibn al-Arabi too refers to seven Abdal.

It is significant that over and over again, the Quran uses the words We, Our, Us. The sense of preservers of the cosmic order can be attributed to these words. Sura xxxvii/164 As-Saffat, Those Who Set the Ranks, reads:

There is not one of Us but hath his known position
Lo! We, even We are They who set the ranks."

The Greeks call al-Khadir, Hormux (Hermes) the adept and Initiator into the Temple Mysteries of the Great Pyramid. Isaiah 19/2 of the old Testament refers to this Pyramid Temple as the "altar to the Lord in the middle of Egypt". Hermes, known to the Arabs as Idris, was called Enoch by the Hebrews.

The Spanish Arab historian Said of Toledo (d. 1069) said:

"Sages affirm that all antediluvian sciences originate with the first Hermes who lived in Said in upper Egypt."

Idris, Enoch, al Khiḍr and Hermes all seem to be one person. This guide al-Khiḍr initiates Moses into deeply esoteric lore. The ijnaj Ilhami, in Hadith traditions, consider al-Khadir as a holy being, mysterious and immortal whom all spiritual initiatory orders revere as the Master of the Path (Tariqa). Al-Khiḍr is often mentioned as the Green Angel Guide in Islamic writings. In fact, in Egyptian frescoes he is some times painted green with the head of an ibis.

Al-Khiḍr can most certainly be connected as the head of the ancient school of the Prophets, el-Khadoras on Mt Carmel (modern Haifa). This sacred mount in mentioned as having been handed back with endowment by Thutmose III in the 1449 B.C. documents which recorded his conquest of the region. He was a great initiate himself. Iamblichus, the Syrian philosopher, calls it the most holy of all mountains, forbidden of access to the profane. The Phophets Elijah, Elisha and Samuel are all recorded to have visited the schools for disciples at Naioth, Bethel and Jericho.

A very valuable text was among others withdrawn by the official circles of the Church from public use. It was the Apocalypse of Elias - a very sacred text of the mystic order of Nazarenes or Essenes, to which order Joseph, Mary, John the Baptist and Jesus himself belonged. Fortunately in 1893 Maspero discovered a Coptic translation of it in the monastic archives of the Brotherhood in Upper Egypt. It gave many details of the school of prophets where the ancient wisdom was imparted at Al Khador.

From Theosophy and Islam, by Theja Gunawardhana

My another books

Sr no.	Book
1	World's Major religions, doctrines and sects
2	An introduction to the Holy Qur'an and it's unsolved mysteries
3	How did humans and language originate ?
4	Islam an introduction and sect
5	Sermons of great people
6	Prayer
7	Allah an introduction
8	Is Al khizr still alive today?
9	Story of harut and marut
10	Grief
11	The mysterious story of Al kahf (Ar raqim)
12	Naming of God
13	Who was Sheeba?
14	Death concept of the Holy Quran

15	What is soul? In view of Religion and science
16	Real Alexander Zulqurnain
17	Where is peace?
18	Origin of ancient religious book, it's author and original copy
19	An introduction to the bible and is the original bible still available today?
20	Does a parallel universe exist?
21	Promise to your self or God?
22	Evidence of God existance
23	Prediction of holy Quran
24	Humanity in the holy Quran?
25	Commandnends of the holy Quran,right or wrong?
26	Similarity in the world famous holy books
27	Is Zulkifl the same Gautam Buddha?
28	Adam to Muhammad
29	Why isolated?

30	For Divorce! Who is responsible?
31	Hadith to denomination
32	Karma is the best?
33	According to dreams, religion and Science
34	End day

<u>All these books are available in Hindi</u> language and other international languages and are also available in e-book for <u>free on Google Play Store</u>.

<u>All the books are available in paper back edition and hard cover edition as well.</u>

<u>These books are also available on Amazon,Flipkart and notionpress.com.</u>

My personal introduction

My name is Abdul Waheed, my father's name is Late Haji Ubaidur Rahman and mother's name is Jaibunnisa. I have liked scientific ideology since childhood and have a calm nature and attachment to books. Due to which my curiosity interest has been continuously used in new discoveries and information. I got selected in polytechnic while doing BSc, but unfortunately it remained incomplete because father and brother died.

Two words of my father, which are very precious for my life,

<u>first - earn honestly, do not take support of lies,</u>

<u>secondly, respect food and eat as much as you want</u>. That's why the education remained incomplete due to the responsibility of the house, then later getting married. Still did not lose courage and

today the book is available in front of you in the form of my thoughts. If any information is left incomplete, please let us know.

Thank you

Contact-

Abdul Waheed,Barabanki, Utter Pradesh, India